HELPING YOUR BRAND-NEW READER

Here's how to make first-time reading easy and fun:

▶ Read the introduction at the beginning of the book aloud. Look through the pictures together so that your child can see what happens in the story before reading the words.

▶ Read the first page to your child, placing your finger under each word.

▶ Let your child touch the words and read the rest of the story. Give him or her time to figure out each new word.

▶ If your child gets stuck on a word, you might say, *"Try something. Look at the picture. What would make sense?"*

▶ If your child is still stuck, supply the right word. This will allow him or her to continue to read and enjoy the story. You might say, *"Could this word be 'ball'?"*

▶ Always praise your child. Praise what he or she reads correctly, and praise good tries too.

▶ Give your child lots of chances to read the story again and again. The more your child reads, the more confident he or she will become.

▶ Have fun!

Text copyright © 2000 by B.G. Hennessy
Illustrations copyright © 2000 by Ana Martín Larrañaga

First edition 2000

Library of Congress Cataloging-in-Publication Data
Hennessy, B. G. (Barbara G.)
Busy Dinah Dinosaur / B. G. Hennessy ;
illustrated by Ana Martín Larrañaga—1st ed.
p. cm. — (Brand new readers)
Summary: More adventures of the playful
dinosaur for beginning readers.
ISBN 0-7636-1140-9
[1. Dinosaurs—Fiction.] I. Martín Larrañaga, Ana, date, ill. II. Title.
PZ7.H3914   Bu 2000
[E]—dc21   00-020928

2 4 6 8 10 9 7 5 3 1

Printed in Hong Kong

This book was typeset in Letraset Arta.
The illustrations were done in watercolor, pastel, and ink.

Candlewick Press
2067 Massachusetts Avenue
Cambridge, Massachusetts 02140

BUSY
DINAH
DINOSAUR

CANDLEWICK PRESS
CAMBRIDGE, MASSACHUSETTS

B.G. Hennessy ILLUSTRATED BY **Ana Martín Larrañaga**

Contents

Dinah's Walk 1

The Pretty Rock 11

Muddy Dinosaurs 21

Good Night, Dinah 31

DINAH'S WALK

Introduction

This story is called *Dinah's Walk*.
It's about all the things Dinah Dinosaur
walks by and then, after she sees
something scary, runs by.

Dinah Dinosaur walks by a volcano.

4

She walks by a big bug.

5

She walks by a waterfall.

6

She sees a T. Rex.

She runs by the waterfall.

8

She runs by the big bug.

She runs by the volcano.

Dinah Dinosaur runs home!

THE PRETTY ROCK

Introduction

This story is called *The Pretty Rock.*
It's about the pretty rock that Dinah
Dinosaur finds and how it turns out
not to be a rock after all.

13

Dinah Dinosaur likes rocks.

"Look at this pretty rock," she says.

She walks around the rock.

She jumps over the rock.

She sits on the rock.

18

The rock moves.

19

Dinah Dinosaur jumps up.

"Look at this pretty turtle," she says.

MUDDY DINOSAURS

Introduction

This story is called *Muddy Dinosaurs.*
It's about how Dinah Dinosaur and her
friend Doug play in the mud until they
are muddy all over and how they get
clean again.

Dinah and Doug play in the mud.

They have mud on their tails.

They have mud on their feet.

They have mud on their faces.

They are muddy dinosaurs.

They jump in the lake.

29

SPLASH!

Dinah and Doug are clean dinosaurs.

GOOD NIGHT, DINAH

Introduction

This story is called *Good Night, Dinah.*
It's about all the things Dinah Dinosaur
does to get ready for bed.

33

The moon is out.

The stars are out.

Dinah is sleepy.

She eats some leaves.

She gets a drink.

She brushes her teeth.

39

She gets in bed.

Good night, Dinah!